Crowded Out
at
SILVER STREET
FARM

Crowded Out
at
SILVER STREET FARM

NICOLA DAVIES
illustrated by Katharine McEwen

WALKER
BOOKS

First published 2012 by Walker Books Ltd
87 Vauxhall Walk, London SE11 5HJ

2 4 6 8 10 9 7 5 3 1

Text © 2012 Nicola Davies
Illustrations © 2012 Katharine McEwen

The right of Nicola Davies and Katharine McEwen to be identified as author and illustrator respectively of this work has been asserted by them in accordance with the Copyright, Designs and Patents Act 1988.

This book has been typeset in Stempel Schneidler and Cows

Printed and bound in Great Britain
by Clays Ltd, St Ives plc

British Library Cataloguing in Publication Data:
a catalogue record for this book is available from the British Library

ISBN 978-1-4063-37822

www.walker.co.uk

For the real Mr Steely, with love

A MAP OF SILVER STREET FARM

Main gate

FLORA'S OFFICE

FLORA'S VAN

Goats

Shee[p]

gate

Duck

N

CANAL

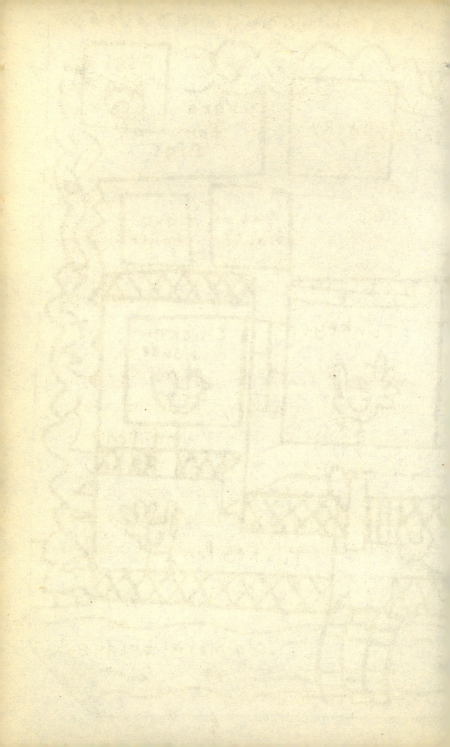

Chapter One

It was one of those days – the sort of day when everything seems to go wrong. The sort of day when cups tip over, string tangles and you can only find one sock.

At Silver Street City Farm, Sputnik, the stupidest of Bobo's lambs, had pushed his way out of his pen five times in an hour; the pigs had escaped and knocked over the churn of goats'

milk and the chickens had got into the office again, and pooed all over the computer.

Meera, Karl and Gemma, the three children who had started Silver Street Farm were racing about, trying to sort out the mishaps, while Flora MacDonald the farm manager rounded up the chickens with the help of her dog Flinty. Just when everyone thought they were getting on top of the chaos, somebody (they never saw who) had left a pet carrier full of guinea pigs in the turkey pen, giving the jittery birds hysterics.

Of course, the Sunday visitors had no idea anything was wrong. They wandered about in the autumn sunshine, watching the goats jumping on the hay bales and the ducks paddling about on the canal; they scratched the backs of the pigs and petted the farm dogs –

Flinty, Buster and Misty. They sat around licking Silver Street ice creams, cakes and biscuits served by Karl's Auntie Nat. And at the end of the afternoon, they all went home with big smiles on their faces, leaving Flora, the children and Auntie Nat to collapse, exhausted, on the old sofas in the farm office, with the dogs at their feet.

For a while, the only sound was the sipping of tea and the crunch of biscuits, but at last Flora gave a big sigh. "The thing is," she said in her broad Scots accent, "we're bursting at the seams."

The children knew that Flora wasn't talking about the effects of Auntie Nat's baking. Silver Street Farm had had a *very* good year. Rather *too* good: so many babies had been born that all the pens and enclosures were quite overcrowded. To add to the problem, visitors had taken to leaving unwanted rabbits and guinea pigs behind; the new arrivals in the turkey pen were not the first.

"It's bad enough finding space for our own animals," Flora grumbled, "without all of Lonchester dumping their unwanted pets on us." She shooed two white rabbits away from her feet and they loped off behind the sofa.

"Not to worry, Flora," said Auntie Nat, shrugging in a particularly Russian sort of way. "Solution is easy. We sell all dumped pets, and some farm animals."

The children exchanged horrified looks. They had worked so hard to get Silver Street started that they couldn't bear the thought of getting rid of *any* animals, even ones that had arrived by mistake!

Right on cue, one of the "dumped pets", a handsomely patterned tortoise, stumped its way across the wooden floor, its feet making little scrapes and thumps as if to protest against Auntie Nat's suggestion.

"You don't want to be sold, do you Rocky?" said Meera to the tortoise.

But Rocky wasn't interested in Meera. He had eyes only for Auntie Nat, and stared at her adoringly.

"Phhh!" said Auntie Nat. "Stupid reptile. What for you look at me?" And she flapped her hand dismissively in Rocky's direction.

The children weren't fooled. They had all seen Auntie Nat scratching Rocky under his wrinkly chin when she thought no one was looking.

"If we sold the rabbits and guinea pigs,"

said Karl innocently, "we'd have to sell Rocky too, Auntie. It's only fair."

"Foolish boy!" Auntie Nat snapped. "Who would want worn out old turtle?"

"I think Rocky is the least of our problems," said Flora. "Auntie Nat's right. Without more space, a lot of animals will have to go."

Karl and Gemma groaned, but Meera had a gleam in her eye that told everyone she'd had "one of her ideas".

"There *is* another solution," Meera said. "We could take over the scrapyard next door. No one ever uses it any more."

Meera's ideas were sometimes a bit mad, but this seemed pretty sensible to the other children.

"Yes," said Karl, catching Meera's enthusiasm, "if we moved all the old cars and stuff, there'd be plenty of room."

"We could have a pets' corner!" exclaimed Gemma delightedly.

But Flora wasn't smiling. "We can't just take it over!" she said, shaking her curls in agitation. "It doesn't belong to us."

"But Silver Street Station didn't belong to us either," said Meera, "and we kind of took it over to make the farm."

"Do you *know* who owns the scrapyard?" Flora asked. "It's Mike Steely, only the richest businessman in Lonchester. He's so secretive, no one even knows where he *lives*. There's no way he'd let us have the scrapyard, even if we could find him to ask. It's just an impossible dream—"

Flora was interrupted by squeals and grunts coming from outside the office door.

"Oh no! The pigs have got out again..." said Karl wearily.

As they all ran out to round up the Gloucester Old Spot sow, Mrs Fattybot, and her piglets, Flora noticed that the gleam in Meera's eyes was brighter still. Words like "no" and "impossible" only made Meera more determined.

Chapter Two

Chinook the Canada goose was restless. In the wild, at this time of year, she would have been flying south with a huge flock of other Canada geese to escape the winter. But Chinook had been hatched at Silver Street and didn't know about migration. All she knew was that ever since the days had begun to get shorter, nothing had felt right. Visits from her best friend

Bish Bosh, the boy who had raised her from an egg, calmed her for a while, but Bish Bosh went to school every day now and sometimes she didn't see him for days.

Chinook hissed at the ducks in irritation as they crowded around her, quacking maddeningly. She poked one in the bottom with her beak and it jumped away in alarm. How satisfying! Then she flapped her wings and paddled the surface of the canal until she had enough speed and lift to fly.

Higher and higher Chinook went, until Silver Street Farm was just a little patchwork pattern in the tangled grey grid of streets, and the canal and the river beyond were two blue ribbons. She was just about to slide away on the wind, when something familiar caught her eye – a tiny red dot moving along the fine grey thread that was the lane down to the farm. It was Bish Bosh coming to see her on his bike! She called out to him, then turned her wings to spill out the air and make a quick descent to meet her friend.

Squirt, Bish Bosh's little brother, was sitting on the bike's pannier rack hanging on for dear life as his brother pedalled with fearless abandon and at toppest top speed towards the Silver Street Farm gates.

"Tell me again, Bish Bosh," said Squirt.

"Flippin' heck, Squirt!" Bish Bosh complained. "I've told you four times already."

"*Please.*"

"*All right!* Franco Lorenzo is in Lonchester with Rene Withers and Richard de Havers to make a film about a magical circus..."

"Yes! Yes!" said Squirt, almost falling off the bike with excitement. "And the next bit too…"

"And they're looking for extras and animals to be in the film."

Squirt really did fall off at this point, and Bish Bosh had to stop and pick his little brother out of the gutter, still babbling with delight about movie stars and famous film directors. But as they were at the gates of Silver Street, it didn't much matter.

"Calm down, Squirt! It's only a stupid film," said Bish Bosh, brushing dirt and bits of crisp out of the smaller boy's hair.

"This could be my big chance, Bish Bosh," said Squirt dreamily. "My first break in the movies!"

Bish Bosh gave his brother a small shove. "Nobody's gonna want *you* in a film."

Squirt looked so downcast that Bish Bosh felt sorry. "Look," he added more kindly, "here's Chinook come to say hello. Any more of your chattering and she'll nip you in the bum. You know how bad-tempered she is just now."

"All right," said Squirt, wiping his nose on the back of his hand. "But can I tell Meera about the filming when we go in?"

Bish Bosh rolled his eyes. "You haven't *still* got a crush on Meera?"

Squirt fell silent, and blushed to the roots of his hair.

Bish Bosh opened the gate to Silver Street Farm, to wheel his bike inside as usual. But instead of groaning slowly outwards like it usually did, the gate swung like a cricket bat, sending Bish

Bosh, the bike, Squirt and Chinook sprawling. Four almost-full-grown pigs shot through the gateway, like ginger and black missiles, with Flora, Gemma, Karl and Meera close behind. The pigs were running as fast as if someone had just told them what bacon was, and the humans struggled to keep up.

Meera ran out of breath first and stopped halfway up the road. "Bish Bosh," she panted, "can you try to head them off on your bike?"

Bish Bosh loved a bike chase. He nodded to Meera and shot off up the road.

"I'll look after Squirt," Meera called after him.

Squirt was delighted. As he and Meera walked back through the farm gates with the dogs wagging their tails, he told her all about Hollywood coming to Lonchester.

Everyone had forgotten about Chinook. She stood in the empty street and looked up at the sky. A moment later she was flying, high up where the horizon called her beyond the boundaries of the city.

Chapter Three

Flora and the children stood at the edge of the biggest roundabout in Lonchester, where roads from all over the city converged and linked up with the motorway. It was very busy, as everyone rushed home from Sundays out and weekends away. The pigs had simply disappeared in the traffic.

"Can anybody see them?" said Flora, standing on tiptoe and peering over the cars.

The children shook their heads.

"Last place I saw them," said Bish Bosh, sliding to a halt on his bike, "was running over the motorway slip road."

Gemma groaned.

"Listen!" said Karl. "I can hear car horns and look, isn't that a police car? I bet that's where the pigs are."

On the other side of the huge roundabout, horns blared out and the blue flashing light of a police car made its way through the traffic.

"If the pigs have caused an accident, we're going to be in so much trouble!" said Flora.

"We could just leave them here and pretend they were nothing to do with us," Bish Bosh said. But seeing the look on Flora's face he added, "Only joking."

"Come on," said Karl grimly. "Let's go and find out what's happened."

It took them a while to make their way safely through the whizzing cars. By the time they reached the other side of the roundabout, two police vehicles were on the scene, with several officers directing the traffic. On the roundabout, which was fenced off with traffic cones, the pigs were happily rooting up flowers that had been the pride of Lonchester Council's gardeners.

A very tall, very fierce-looking police officer walked up to Flora.

"Oh dear," Flora breathed. "Oh dearie dear!"

"Are these your animals, miss?" said the officer, in a voice so loud and stern that Flora, who was normally very confident, found that she'd lost her voice. She nodded.

"These animals have caused a severe obstruction to traffic," the officer continued.

"They have damaged council property. They are in breach of regulation seven two five, section eight, *and* regulation three five nine, subsections 12, 13 and 25. You and your animals, miss, will be leaving this location in police custody. Do I make myself clear?"

It was all looking rather grim for the Silver Streeters when two Things happened.

The first Thing was a large hand. It landed on the officer's shoulder and a familiar voice said, "My young friends here giving you grief, PC Tydie?"

The children sighed with relief. It was Sergeant Short, Silver Street's best friend in the Lonchester police department!

PC Tydie seemed to shrink. "These people and their animals," he spluttered, "have breached regulations—"

"Yes, yes, I'm sure they have," Sergeant Short interrupted kindly. "But really is there any point clogging up the courts with three kids and some pigs when we could be catching real criminals?"

Before PC Tydie had a chance to answer, the second Thing happened: a tanned, silver-haired man in a suit got out of a shiny limousine with tinted windows. He took off his sunglasses, smiled broadly at the two police officers and shook each of them by the hand. "Franco Lorenzo," he said, introducing himself, although by the starstruck looks on the faces around him, he must have known an introduction wasn't really needed.

His soft American accent reminded Meera of a cat purring. A very big, confident cat. A tiger, perhaps.

"I'm very sorry that some of my cast have been causing you trouble," said Mr Lorenzo with a neon smile.

Franco Lorenzo's cast? The three children and Flora looked at each other in amazement.

"Yes, these animals and children are appearing in my film," Mr Lorenzo continued smoothly. He waved his hand elegantly at a Land Rover and trailer that had suddenly appeared out of nowhere. "My people will take care of the pigs," he said. "Of course, I will cover the cost of any damage and, if you will allow me, I will see these young people safely home."

The children had never seen their friend Sergeant Short flustered before. He managed to say, "Thankyouverymuch."

But PC Tydie just opened his mouth like a goldfish and nothing at all came out.

The pigs were rounded up onto the trailer while Flora and the children got into the shiny limousine with the most famous film director in the world!

Bish Bosh chuckled quietly to himself. "When Squirt hears about this, he's gonna kill me!"

Chapter Four

"Bish Bosh will kill me for this!" said Squirt. "I shouldn't have let her fly off!"

"Chinook quite often flies off on her own, Squirt," said Meera.

"Not for this long," Squirt whined. "And now it's getting dark. She never stays away this long."

"She'll be fine," said Meera. "Stop worrying! Just pass me another guinea."

Meera and Squirt had tried to solve at least one of their overcrowding problems by setting up a guinea-pig pen in the office. The guinea pigs really liked their new home. They ran about on the fresh straw and made little conversational squeaks to each other. The only snag was that Flora's desk was right in the middle of the pen.

"Flora will just have to be careful not to tread on them," said Meera. "Can you put the last ones in while I see if I can find a phone number for Mike Steely?"

"You can't just ring him up!" said Squirt.

But Meera wasn't listening. She was staring at Flora's computer screen and muttering to herself.

As Squirt put the last wriggling rodent into the pen, Auntie Nat walked in with a tray of tea and biscuits. "In South America," she said, putting the tray down on one of the sofas, "guinea pigs are food. They live on kitchen floor, then whoosh, straight into oven."

Squirt stared at her in shocked silence.

"Why you look at me like this?" Auntie Nat shrugged. "I only tell you truth. Lucky for you I have no guinea-pig recipe. But look, the dogs already read South American recipe book, eh?"

Misty, Flinty and Buster had pushed their noses through the wire to sniff the guinea pigs hungrily.

"They are *not* the same as rats!" Squirt told the dogs. "You aren't allowed to eat them!"

Meera climbed back out of the guinea-pig pen and sat down, staring at her phone with a rather dazed expression on her face.

"I definitely need a cup of tea," she said. "I've just had a text from Flora. They're on their way back with the pigs … and Franco Lorenzo!"

"Squirt!" exclaimed Auntie Nat. "Stop jumping on sofa. Tea will spill!"

Franco Lorenzo perched elegantly on the edge of one of the Silver Street sofas and nibbled on a bit of Auntie Nat's drizzle cake. He was explaining how he came to the rescue of the Silver Streeters from PC Tydie.

"I am very intuitive," he said. "I read the situation immediately: escaped animals, very angry policeman, young people being bullied. Simple. I just *had* to come and help."

"Well, we're very grateful, Mr Lorenzo," said Flora, who in spite of all her determination to be Very Sensible with someone Extremely Famous in her office, found a rather silly smile spreading over her face.

Mr Lorenzo went on. "But you know Miss

MacDonald, I was not being entirely the Good Samaritan." Mr Lorenzo put down his teacup and turned his gaze like a spotlight on all the Silver Streeters in the room. "You see," he continued, "my film is called *The Magic Circus*: it's all about a magic place – part circus, part farm, part Noah's ark – where animals live with gnomes and fairies and an enchanted child and his parents."

Gemma, Karl and Meera thought it sounded a bit silly, but they were much too polite to say so, especially when Mr Lorenzo added, "So I would like to have your animals in my movie: your pigs and sheep and goats and these um little … what are they?"

"Guinea pigs, Mr Lorenzo," said Squirt, smiling like a freshly polished sun.

"Ah, I see. And of course I will pay for their hire."

Flora's smile was no longer silly. Mr Lorenzo was offering them a way out of their overcrowding situation, if only for a short time. It could even be a way of earning enough money for Silver Street to buy more space. She thought longingly of the junkyard next door... "Yes, Mr Lorenzo," she said. "I'm sure we can come to a mutually satisfactory arrangement."

"Wonderful!" Mr Lorenzo laughed. "If you could lend some of your young helpers to help take care of the animals, Miss MacDonald, while we film, that would be so much the better."

Out of the corner of her eye, Flora could see Squirt almost exploding with excitement.

Everyone was smiling as they went out into the yard to say goodbye to Mr Lorenzo.

Almost everyone. Bish Bosh stood apart

from the group of waving children and adults. He looked up into the dark sky and wondered if he would ever see his friend Chinook again.

The next day, the whole of Lonchester was buzzing with movie fever. All the newspapers were full of it.

"HOLLYWOOD COMES TO LONCHESTER," announced *The Lonchester Herald*.

"LONCHESTER – THE NEW LA," said *The City Gazette*.

"OUR CITY STEALS THE SCENE," said *The Daily Post*.

Only *The Lonchester Sun* had heard about Mr Lorenzo and the pigs on the roundabout. But their reporter hadn't quite got the story straight and the headline was: "PIGS ATTACK FILM DIRECTOR IN SUNDAY TRAFFIC HORROR."

Rockin' Roland Rogers, Lonchester City FM's most famous DJ, had more calls on his phone-in than ever before...

"Sooo, let's hear from Molly in the north of the city right next to the old castle ruins where the filming is all happening..." drawled Roland.

"It's so exciting!" Molly yelled. "All the winnydoogoos and that have been arriving and I think I saw Richard de Havers in one of them limerines."

"One *very* excited Lonchester citizen there," said Roland. "I think she means Winnebagos, those big motor homes, and limousines. Let's go to line two now … Josh is down by the canal, I believe."

"Hi, Roland! Everybody needs to switch on their telly, right? Cos, like, that movie company, yeah? They're, like, stealing the animals from the city farm! And Cosmic TV are filming it."

"Thanks for that, Josh," said Roland. "Not quite sure what you're talking about, but if you do turn on Cosmic TV … just make sure to keep your *radio* tuned right here. Now, let's have some tunes: here's the latest release from The Antarctic Funkies…"

Of course, like the reporter from *The Lonchester Sun*, Josh hadn't quite got his story straight. Animals *were* leaving Silver Street Farm in a 21st Century Sox truck, but they were about to leave for the film set just outside town. Sashi and Stewy, Silver Street's old friends from Cosmic TV, were there to cover the story for the morning news.

Sashi, the reporter, was interviewing the children. "So, how did you choose the animals for the movie?" she asked.

Out of the corner of her eye, Meera saw Squirt opening his mouth to speak. She knew he'd say something like: *we chose the ones who escape most.* Which would be true, but not really what anyone wanted Mr Lorenzo to hear. So, quick as a flash, Meera kicked Squirt in the ankle.

Unfortunately, Karl had been thinking the same as Meera, so Squirt got kicked in both ankles. While he was recovering, Meera pitched in with an answer. "We chose the animals who have character," said Meera, beaming into the camera. Which was true because character didn't mean "good" or "nice" or "well behaved".

"And star quality," said Karl, because the demanding, diva-like behaviour of Mrs Fattybot was very like some famous actresses he'd heard of.

"And intelligence!" Gemma added, which was a *bit* true. Bobo *was* intelligent – that was why she was so good at escaping – but her two lambs didn't have a brain cell between them.

"Well thank you, Silver Street," said Sashi, winding up. "In addition to the animals, some Silver Street humans could end up as movie stars too. These young people have been released from school to be on set with their animals for a whole week! That's it from Cosmic TV Early News. Tune in again at midday."

The red light went off on the camera.

"Thanks for that, guys," said Sashi. "So is it just you four going on set with the animals? Not Bish Bosh too?"

The children shook their heads.

"Chinook's gone missing," said Squirt a bit sheepishly. "He wants to be here in case she comes back."

"And he can help Flora," said Karl.

Stewy the cameraman grinned widely. "She won't need much help. You're taking all the naughtiest animals with you!" he said. "Especially those two goats – Zelda and Arkady. They bite a hole in me every time I film 'em!"

Meera, Karl and Gemma exchanged guilty smiles.

Chapter Six

The truck with the Silver Street Farm animals and children on board, wound its way across the grounds of Lonchester Castle to the set of *The Magic Circus*. It looked like complete chaos to Meera. A huge, bright green big top sat like a fat spider in the middle of a web of huts, smaller tents and camper vans, cars, cables and lights. An enormous number of people were all dashing about looking worried. There was a lot of noise – shouting, the hum of generators and the *beep beep beep* of trucks reversing.

When the truck arrived at the tent where the Silver Street animals were going to live during the film shoot, two gangling young men came to greet them.

"G'day kids," said the taller of the two. "I'm Tel and this here's Barry, my little brother."

The shorter gangly one smiled and pointed first at Tel's chest and then at his own. "Australians, us," he said.

"Yeah, I think they might have got that from the accent, Barry." Tel smiled. "We're the animal handlers on this shoot," he continued. "So whatever you need, we're here to help."

"Yep." Barry nodded. "Help. That's the word."

*   *   *

Even with the two Australians' help, the Silver Street animals did not behave as well coming out of the truck as they had on the way in. Mrs Fattybot and Bobo managed to do a couple of circuits of the tent before going into their pens. Sputnik was only prevented from running under a van delivering sandwiches by Barry diving to grab his back legs.

"Used to be quite a good rugby player, our Barry," Tel commented as his brother tackled the young ram.

It took more than an hour to get all the animals safely in their spacious new quarters. Only the guinea pigs were quiet and easy to handle.

"Phew," said Tel, pushing a hand through his spiky hair. "Bit lively, your lot!"

"Yep," said Barry. "Lively."

"Do you think they'll be OK when it comes to filming?" Meera asked nervously.

"Oh yep," said Tel. "We'll see 'em right. No worries."

Meera wasn't convinced, but as Tel and Barry wanted to introduce them to the animal star of the film, there wasn't time for worrying.

"Come on, guys," said Tel. "Come meet our superstar, Margie!"

The children turned to see an elephant standing in the concrete yard just outside the tent. Its huge grey bulk filled the entrance.

"Wow! An elephant!" said all the children together.

A slight woman with a thick plait shining white against her dark skin stood at the elephant's side.

"That's Ruma," said Tel. "She's Margie's mahut. That means keeper. Only lady mahut in the whole world. She's awesome."

"Awesome," said Barry quietly.

Ruma beckoned to them. "Come and say hello." She smiled.

None of the children had ever been close to an elephant before. Margie was huge, but the look in her brown eyes was so friendly that the children weren't afraid. Margie lifted her trunk towards them.

"She'll use her trunk to get to know you," Ruma told them. "She won't hurt you."

Meera held her breath as Margie's trunk reached for her. She could look right down the twin nostrils like a big rubber pipe and smell the composty scent of Margie's breath. Margie breathed in Meera's smell and touched her face

and hair with the little fleshy finger on the tip of her trunk. It was amazing how delicate and gentle that big muscly trunk was.

Margie sniffed and touched each of the children in turn, but when she got to Squirt, she seemed quite fascinated. She rubbed his hair and pulled at his t-shirt so that it tickled and made Squirt laugh.

"Perhaps," Ruma said, "you would like to help me bathe her?"

The children looked round at Tel and Barry.

"Go for it!" said Tel. "We'll feed your animals. Not every day you get to bath an elephant!"

"Nope," said Barry. "Not every day."

Ruma gave Meera, Karl and Gemma a brush each – the kind you use to sweep straw off a farmyard – and Squirt lived up to

his name and held the hose pipe. He sprayed Margie with water and the others brushed her wet skin. Margie loved it and made deep, contented, rumbling sounds. Ruma got her to lift each of her feet in turn so they too could be thoroughly wetted and brushed.

As he scrubbed at the underside of Margie's right front foot, Karl noticed how the elephant shifted her weight onto the other three feet.

Ruma smiled. "Elephants are very light on their feet, like dancers," she told him. "When they walk in sand, they hardly leave a mark."

Once Margie's body was clean, it was time to brush her teeth. Squirt directed the hose into her pink mouth, while Ruma scrubbed her teeth and stumpy tusks with a giant toothbrush. Finally, Margie was given a big bucket of water to drink. She dipped in her trunk and the water

disappeared. Then she put the end of her trunk in her mouth and let the water run down her throat. But she saved a little bit and just as Squirt picked up the empty bucket, she sprayed water all over him. Everyone, including Squirt, burst out laughing.

"She really likes you." Ruma laughed. "She only plays tricks on people she really, really likes."

A hundred metres away, Franco Lorenzo was having a very bad day indeed. He'd just heard that Sky Malone, the famous child actor who was to be the star of *The Magic Circus*, had chickenpox. The cost of postponing filming for the time it would take Sky to recover made Franco feel so sick that he had to open the door of his Winnebago and take a few breaths of fresh air. Which is how he came to see his other co-star, Margie the elephant, squirting a skinny little kid with water from her trunk. Even from a distance, Franco could see the cute way the kid laughed.

"Margie," Franco breathed, "I think you have an eye for talent. Maybe we don't need to postpone filming after all."

Chapter Seven

Meera decided that being on a film set was a very weird mixture of fun and boring. It had been fun hanging out with Ruma and Margie, Tel and Barry, sleeping in their very own caravan and putting on the green gnome costumes they had to wear for filming. And it had been fun watching the big top fill up with all kinds of animals. As well as the Silver Street pigs and goats, sheep, rabbits and guinea pigs, there were alpacas – creatures that Meera had always wished they could have at Silver Street – and zoo animals like zebras and camels. There was even one rather ancient-looking lion on a chain. Once the animals were in place, the actors and the acrobats had arrived, dressed in fantastic costumes and doing backflips whenever they wanted.

But that had all been hours ago. Now Meera was bored of trying to hold Arkady and Zelda in one place with their halters, to stop them from nibbling the alpacas in the pen next door.

Cameras zoomed over them on wires and around them on little rails, back and forth, again and again, and people rushed about with clipboards and electrical equipment, speaking very fast and treating all the animal handlers in gnome costumes as if they simply didn't exist.

Gemma and Karl were taking care of the pigs and sheep in pens over on the other side of the tent, and Squirt had been taken off guinea-pig duty to do something mysterious with Ruma and Margie.

So, as the lady with the alpacas only spoke Italian, Meera had no one to talk to. And in spite of all her efforts to distract Zelda and Arkady from nibbling things they shouldn't, the goats had managed to bite bits out of her gnome jacket.

"OK, everybody," said someone through a loud hailer, "take twenty."

That, Meera knew, meant a break. She was just wondering if it would be OK to leave the goats alone for five minutes, when Gemma and Karl came rushing towards her.

"Meera, you've got to come right now..." said Gemma, out of breath with excitement.

"Yes, right now," Karl echoed. "Mr Lorenzo's giving Squirt a screen test with Margie!"

"And if he passes," Gemma continued, "he's going to be the star of the film!"

Meera wasn't absolutely sure what a screen test was, but it was obviously pretty important. It would just *have* to be OK to leave the goats for a moment or two.

Sputnik was cross. The crossness buzzed in his small brain like an irritating bee. Why had the humans moved him from that nice big pen in the tent to this small one? The buzzing got worse. He wanted to bash something, very very much...

Mrs Fattybot's four grown-up children milled about in their pen. There was nowhere interesting to root about, and no mud wallow to snooze in. They didn't know where they wanted to be, but more and more, it wasn't here…

Sean the cockerel and his little group of wives clucked and scratched in their enclosure, ignoring all the noise and bustle around them. But the camera swooping overhead looked like a hawk. It made Sean nervous – very, very nervous…

Zelda and Arkady liked to taste new things. And the new things they most wanted to taste were the creatures in the pen next door to them. All morning, they had tried to get close for a nibble of their fluffy wool, but Meera had pulled their halters and stopped them. But now that Meera was gone…

Squirt's heart was beating so hard that he thought he might just die. Mr Lorenzo was giving him a screen test, to see if he could act well enough to replace Sky Malone. If he did well, all his dreams would come true. Everyone on the set had come to watch. Hundreds of pairs of eyes were looking at him. Squirt knew that the whole of his life depended on the next few minutes, on walking up to Margie and saying, "My name's Ben. Will you be my friend?" But he felt frozen to the spot.

And then the clapperboard snapped in front of his face and someone yelled, "Action!" It was now or never. Squirt looked at Margie and her small, brown eye looked back. Suddenly, he felt quite calm. He stepped forward into his dream, which felt as easy and as natural as breathing.

*　　*　　*

Back inside the tent, the technician decided that this break would be a good time to test cameras. He pushed a button and sent one skimming low over the pens.

Sean glanced up and saw the camera coming right for him and his girls. People say chickens can't fly, but a mixture of flapping, jumping and sheer blind fury launched Sean high enough in the air to grab the camera with his feet. He pecked its glass eye like a road drill.

Below, the screeching of the hens made Sputnik snap. He crashed his head into the side of his pen, so hard that the sheep pen and the pigpen next door came down like a pack of cards.

Mrs Fattybot, never the sort of pig to stay calm in a crisis, went straight for all out panic.

She tossed aside the fencing that had fallen on her back and accelerated like a racing car across the floor of the big top.

Her piggy panic was highly infectious: her four children caught it instantly and raced after her at even higher speed, trailing bits of fencing behind them. The alpacas weren't quite at panic point, but when Zelda and Arkady pulled free of the pole they were tied to and reached for a nibble of their wool, they lost it. The pole clattered into their pen, and the alpacas leapt their fence and joined the piggy sprint, followed by Arkady and Zelda, the miniature ponies, the zebra and a gang of guinea pigs. The whole stampeding herd burst out of the big top just as Squirt's screen test was almost done.

Margie saw the panicking animals heading towards her, about to trample her small new friend. She wound her trunk around his waist and snatched him to safety above her head.

Meera, along with all the other humans, leapt out of the way of the stampede. She launched herself into the air and had a split-second to think, "When I hit the ground, it's really going to hurt!"

But something broke Meera's fall. Two somethings in fact. She opened her eyes and found that she had landed on Mr Lorenzo and another man who looked very like him, but with a less rumply suit. Meera got ready to talk herself out of a lot of trouble, but it looked like she didn't need to. Both men were laughing. Mr Lorenzo, in fact, seemed delighted.

"Well, I won't have to stage the stampede scene now! I just kept the camera running and I've got it for real!" Mr Lorenzo laughed. *"And* we have a new star for our movie! The kid is terrific. I must go and congratulate him." He scrambled to his feet and rushed off.

The Mr Lorenzo lookalike and Meera helped each other up.

"Sorry I landed on you!" said Meera.

"No problem. Things like this always happen on my bro— I mean, Franco's film shoots," said the man.

"I'm Meera, by the way," said Meera, sticking out her hand to shake.

"Pleased to meet you," said the man. "I'm Mike, Mike Steely."

Meera's eyes gleamed like little fires. "Mr Steely," she said. "I'm *so* glad to meet you."

Chapter Eight

Back at the farm, Flora and Bish Bosh were trying to make a bit more room in the pens by cutting back the weeds. Bish Bosh found that he could almost forget about Chinook if he got really fierce with a patch of nettles.

"Look how much bigger this pen is now!" said Flora, standing back to admire their work.

"Now the nettles are gone," said Bish Bosh, slashing with his stick, "we can see through the fence into the scrapyard."

Flora laughed. "Don't show Meera, Bish Bosh. It'll make her even more determined."

"Talk of the devil," said Bish Bosh, looking over Flora's shoulder, "she's here!"

A very excited Meera, Gemma and Karl were walking across the yard to the pigpen with someone who looked like Franco Lorenzo's less handsome twin.

"Aren't you supposed to be making a film?" said Bish Bosh.

"Well," said Karl, "there's – um – a bit of a break in filming today."

"We'll explain later," said Gemma.

"We've brought someone to meet you, Flora," said Meera. "This is Mr Steely."

"I hear you have a few overcrowding problems, Miss MacDonald." Mike smiled.

*   *   *

Everyone talked over cups of tea in the farm office. To the children's astonishment, it turned out that Flora had been having "impossible dreams" about the scrapyard all along. She climbed through the guinea-pig pen to her desk and pulled out some plans that showed what the scrapyard would look like if it became part of Silver Street Farm.

Mike stared at the plans in silence. Meera, Karl and Gemma held their breath. Would he decide to give them the scrapyard?

Suddenly, Auntie Nat burst in. "You have heard news? Squirt is going to be big star!" she announced excitedly.

"What?" said Flora and Bish Bosh together, looking at Karl, Gemma and Meera.

"Sorry…" said Gemma.

"We were just about to tell you…" said Karl.

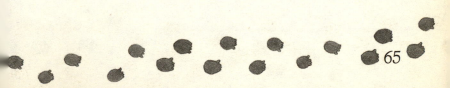

Auntie Nat handed Bish Bosh *The City Gazette*. A picture of Squirt and Margie took up most of the front page.

"LOCAL ORPHAN TO BE HOLLYWOOD STAR!"

Bish Bosh was speechless, smiling a huge smile, but also looking like he might burst into tears. The Silver Streeters gathered round him in a comforting huddle.

Mike was quite forgotten, until a few moments later when the children turned around to find him holding Rocky and looking at his shell very closely. "I don't believe it!" he said. "Where did you get this tortoise?"

"Somebody just dumped it on us," said Flora. "Just like the guinea pigs."

Mike looked incredibly pleased. "This is Motty," he said, grinning and shaking his head. "He's a very, very rare kind of tortoise –

a Ploughshare tortoise from Madagascar. My hobby is breeding them. That's one reason why I keep quiet about where I live. But two years ago, somebody found my house and stole Motty. I've been looking for him ever since." He planted a kiss on the top of the tortoise's shell.

"I've missed you old son!" he said. And everyone laughed, except for Auntie Nat.

Motty seemed to seal the deal. Mike said that he had almost forgotten he owned the old scrapyard. He wouldn't miss it, he said, but there was just one condition...

"I think you can see that Franco and I are related," he explained. "But I like a quiet life with my tortoises when I'm not working, so I don't let on that he's my brother – my half brother. His mum's from New York and my mum was a Lonchester girl. I'd really appreciate it if you helped me keep that secret. I don't want the papers to know."

"That's like me and Squirt," Bish Bosh whispered to Karl. "Except we had the same mum, but different dads."

Flora shook Mr Steely's hand.

"Yes, of course," she said. "Your secret is safe with us."

Mike took all the children back to the film set, so Bish Bosh could see Squirt and so the others could try to keep the Silver Street animals out of any more trouble. Flora and Auntie Nat waved them off.

"I'm sorry about Rocky," Flora said. "I know you were fond of him."

"Phhff," Auntie Nat said, with a very unconvincing shrug. "I don't care about stupid old turtle."

Chapter Nine

Everyone on set loved Squirt, even his two grown-up co-stars – Rene Withers and Richard de Havers – who played his parents in the film and who were famous for not liking anyone but themselves. He learnt his lines, he worked hard and all his scenes with Margie went smoothly. Mr Lorenzo said that he had never had a shoot go so well. They finished filming in record time and a whole week ahead of schedule.

To everyone's great surprise, Squirt turned up the very next day with Bish Bosh for Saturday farm chores, just like always. And just like always, he rode on Bish Bosh's pannier rack, although now Bish Bosh had a new and very shiny bike.

"It was brilliant, the filming and all," Squirt said, "and I expect I'll have to go to America sometime, but I'll always want to come back here to Silver Street."

"That's if we'll still have you, Squirt," said Bish Bosh, ruffling his brother's hair.

"Of course we will," said Meera, but no one noticed how this made Squirt blush, because at that moment a huge digger and an enormous Twentieth Century Sox truck rolled into the Silver Street yard, setting Buster, Flinty and Misty barking madly.

The back of the truck opened and out of it came Ruma and then Margie. The three dogs stopped barking at once. They had never seen an animal so huge and they lay down in a row in the yard, completely overwhelmed. After Ruma and Margie, came several men with toolkits, wearing hard hats and overalls. It took the children a moment to recognize Tel and Barry, Franco Lorenzo and Mike Steely amongst them.

"G'day!" Tel grinned at the children. "Bet you thought you'd seen the last of us, eh?"

"Yep, last of us!" Barry beamed.

Flora turned to Franco and Mike, quite speechless.

"I'm paying these guys for another week," Franco explained, "so they might as well do some work."

"We can get the scrapyard cleared this morning," said Mike. "Then some of my contractors will be here this afternoon to do fences and make a start on whatever animal enclosures you need."

"And Margie will help," Ruma chipped in. "She is keen to do some physical work. She trained as a forestry elephant, so she's very good at lifting things."

"Don't worry, Miss MacDonald." Mike smiled his most film-starry kind of smile. "My brother and I are taking care of all the costs. After all Silver Street has done for us, it's the least we can do."

"Oh and Meera, you know those alpacas you liked so much?" Franco grinned. "Well, they'll be coming to live at Silver Street Farm next week."

Everyone laughed, but Gemma and Karl most of all. They hardly ever saw their friend lost for words.

The digger made quick work of breaking the old chain-link fence that divided the scrapyard from Silver Street Farm. Then it loaded the rusted cars onto a truck and scraped away the tough bushes and brambles and piles of rocks and rubble. Margie stacked the old railway sleepers into a pile, ready to be made into fences and huts, and the children collected all the smaller bits of rubbish and scrap that littered the yard.

At lunchtime, Auntie Nat made them all come into the office for sandwiches and huge mugs of tea. Everyone was in such good spirits, it felt like a party. Margie wanted to join in. She put her trunk in through the window and Auntie Nat gave her cakes.

In the afternoon, Mike's men joined in and brought a huge roll of wire, a pile of posts and a machine to pop the posts into the ground. In no time at all, a smart new fence had been set up around the cleared space. For the first time, Flora and the children could see just how big new Silver Street was going to be.

"It's a lot bigger than I thought!" said Flora.

"It's more than twice as big!" exclaimed Meera.

"We can have pens with proper grass for grazing!" said Gemma.

"And an even bigger mud wallow for the pigs!" said Karl.

"It can't all be done today!" said Mike, with a big smile.

"But we could have new pens for the film-star animals, couldn't we?" asked Meera. "It's been very stressful for them in that big tent with all those lights and things."

Mike grinned. "You're a very determined person, aren't you, Meera?"

"That's *one* word for it!" said Gemma.

"*We* usually just say 'mad'!" said Karl.

The bright autumn afternoon came to an end. The Silver Street film stars, or at least the four-legged ones, were in big new pens in the newest bit of Silver Street Farm. In the old part of Silver Street, people, equipment and an elephant were being loaded back into the truck, on the first leg of some very, very long journeys.

From the far end of the old scrapyard, Bish Bosh watched as everyone said their goodbyes – shaking hands, hugging, promising to keep in touch. He saw his little brother hugging Ruma, then Franco and finally twining in Margie's trunk. His heart turned over, and he wished he had had the chance to say goodbye to Chinook.

He looked up into the pink-streaked sky, to keep the tears from escaping from his eyes, and saw a familiar shape high above him. Then more, just like it. He rubbed his eyes, but he wasn't seeing things, because now he could hear their voices as they slid down the wind to land. Chinook! His beloved bird had come home at last and brought with her a whole new family – her very own flock!

Chinook landed just a metre or so away and ran towards Bish Bosh dipping her head and peeping, greeting him in goose style. The twenty other Canada geese she'd brought with her did just the same, so Bish Bosh was surrounded by a calling, flapping, goose gang, dancing in the rosy dusk.

Up by the truck, everyone stopped their goodbyes to watch.

"Where's a camera when you need one?" breathed Franco.

Mike shook his head in wonder. "Do things like this always happen at Silver Street?" he asked.

"All the time," Meera smiled, "all the time."

The Little Farm in the Big City

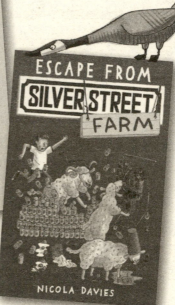

SPRING FEVER AT
SILVER STREET FARM
NICOLA DAVIES

ALL ABOARD AT
SILVER STREET FARM
NICOLA DAVIES

CROWDED OUT AT
SILVER STREET FARM
NICOLA DAVIES

FROZEN SOLID AT
SILVER STREET FARM
NICOLA DAVIES